This book belongs to

....

WONDERSHOP
AT TARGET

Copyright © 2019

make believe ideas ltd

The Wilderness, Berkhamsted, Hertfordshire, HP4 2AZ, UK.
501 Nelson Place, P.O. Box 141000, Nashville, TN 37214-1000, USA.

www.makebelieveideas.com

Written by Rosie Greening.

LLaMa's CHRISTMAS GifT

Written by Rosie Greening

make believe ideas

In the distant **misty mountains** lived a **llama** with a skill:
he could **balance things** upon his back
to give his friends a **thrill!**

But Llama **never** used this gift in any **helpful** way.
Instead, he carried **silly** things to **show off** every day.

One **Christmas**, Llama's parents needed help to **trim the tree**. But **Llama** had a different plan, and shouted:

"Look at MEeeeee!"

He **heaved** the tree upon his back

to **balance** in a flash,

then **tripped**

on all the **fairy lights**

and **fell down** with a . . .

They said, **"You need a job where you can USE your gift instead."**

They gave Llama a **flyer** with a **job posting** that said . . .

FAIRYTALE FOREST

HELP WANTED

It's very nearly **Christmas**,
and there's so much **work** to do.
So **hurry** to the **forest**,
and we'll find the **job** for **YOU!**

Call 555-JINGLE to apply

He said **goodbye** to everyone,

then **trotted** on his way,

toward the place where **Santa's teams**
prepared for **Christmas Day**.

FAIRYTALE FOREST,
NORTH POLE ➤

As **Christmas Eve** was dawning, Llama spied an **elf** ahead.

"Are you here about a **job?** I'll find you one," she said.

She put him in the **Toy Team,**

who built **perfect things** each day.

But he found it much too **fiddly,**

so the team **sent him away.**

Next, he tried the **Trim Team,**
who **hung garlands** up with ease.
But Llama was no **squirrel,**
so he **couldn't climb the trees!**

Llama moved from **team to team,**
but **nothing** fit the bill.

In **every job,**

he found the same:

he didn't have the **skill!**

"**I'm useless!**" mumbled Llama,

feeling miserable and small.

"I thought that I was **gifted**,

but **I can't do this at all!**"

He **wandered** through the **forest**,

having **nowhere else** to go.

Then all at once, he saw a **flash**

of **color** in the **snow**…

"**They're Christmas gifts!**" cried Llama,
as he spotted **more** and **more**.
"**Someone** must have **lost** them here:
I wonder who they're for?"

He **picked up** all the **presents** and **piled** them on his **back,** then **followed** all the **gifts along** the **winding forest track.**

At last, the **trail** led Llama to a little **reindeer crew**,

a **sleigh stuffed** full of **presents**...

... and a **worried Santa** too!

Llama trotted up to him

and shyly said, **"Hello!**

**Do these gifts belong to you?
I found them in the snow!"**

"**Thank you,** Llama," Santa said.
"They **fell out** on the way.

But we have so many **gifts** this **year**,
they won't fit in the sleigh!"

In an instant, **Llama** knew his **skills** could be the **key**.
He cried out,
"**I can carry them –**
just pass those gifts to me!"

He piled up

every present

and as *Santa*

watched in shock,

the tower **grew**...

and **grew**...

but stayed as **steady** as a **rock!**

With **everything** packed up **at last,**
the **sleigh**
WHOOSHEd
through the air,

and the team **delivered** all the **gifts** to houses **everywhere.**

"You saved the day,"

said Santa.

"Now how can I help you?"

"I'd like a job," said Llama,

"but there's nothing I can do!"

"**Of course there is!**" said Santa.
"You **proved yourself** tonight.
With such **amazing balance skills**,
you need a **job** that's **right!**"

Santa found the **llama**

an **extremely** special **role:**

transporting **piles** of **things**

to all the **teams** around the **Pole!**

So **Llama** made his **parents proud**
and **proved** what he could do.
He **learned** to use his **gifts** for **good**
and be **more useful** too!

MERRY Christmas

FAIRYTALE FOREST

Mr. & Mrs. Llama

Wooly Way

Misty Mountains

EMPLOYEE OF THE YEAR

Wish you were here!